DONATED BY
WALLBURG PTO

disc

Messengers of Rain

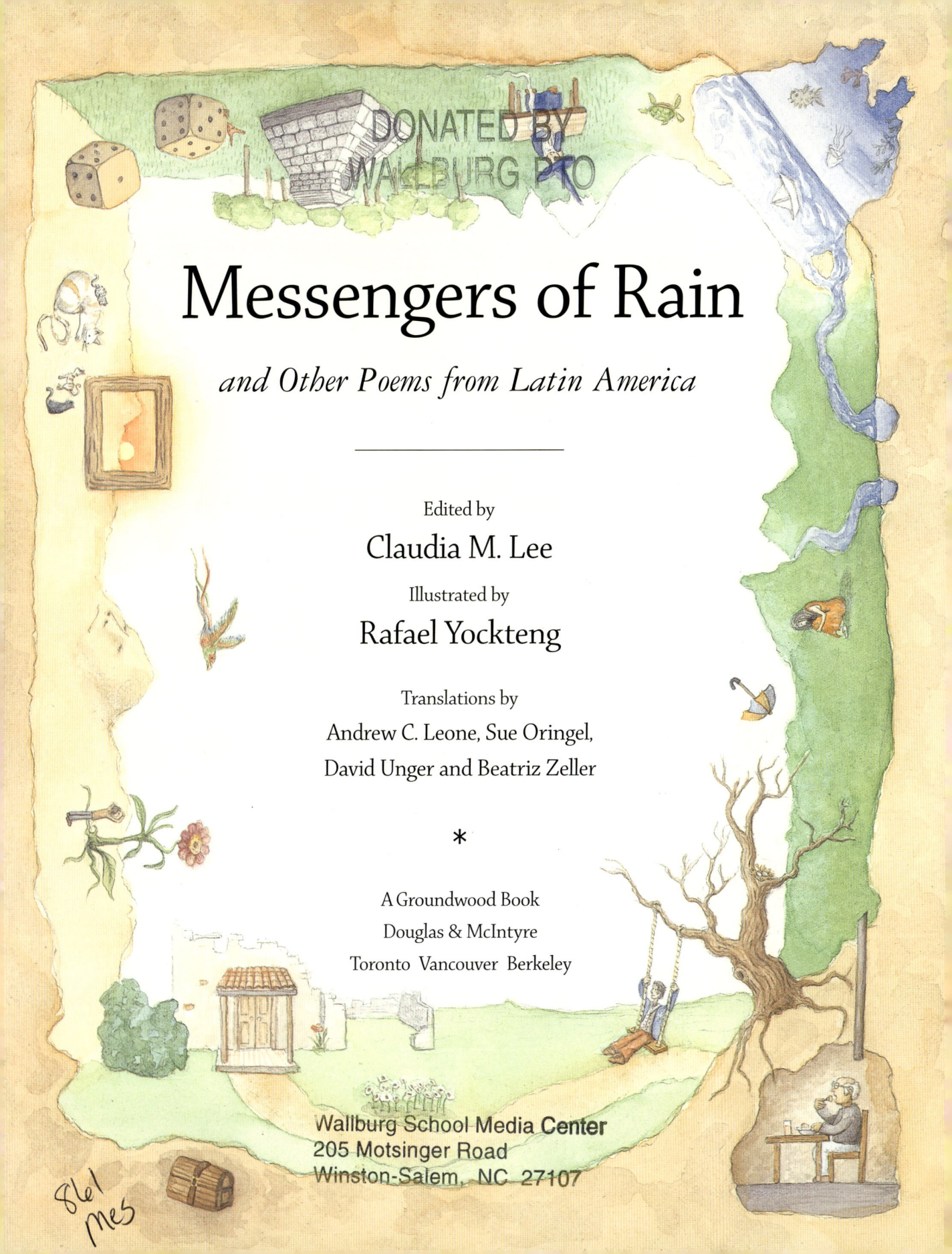

Messengers of Rain

and Other Poems from Latin America

Edited by
Claudia M. Lee

Illustrated by
Rafael Yockteng

Translations by
Andrew C. Leone, Sue Oringel,
David Unger and Beatriz Zeller

*

A Groundwood Book
Douglas & McIntyre
Toronto Vancouver Berkeley

Acknowledgments

I would like to thank my partner, José Antonio Ramírez, and my children, Juan Martín, Natalia and Ana Camila, who give me kisses and smiles every day. I would like to thank Andrew C. Leone, Sue Oringel, David Unger and Beatriz Zeller, who used their ability with words and feeling for two cultures to translate the poems into English. I would also like to acknowledge the generous collaborations received from Enrique Solano Rodríguez and Javier Villegas Fernández from Peru, Sergio Andricaín and Anne C. Doherty from the United States, Claudia Ferreira Talero from Nicaragua, Magali Leal de Urdaneta from Venezuela and, of course, Patricia Aldana, Nan Froman, Lucy Fraser and Michael Solomon from Groundwood Books, who shaped this collection from beginning to end.

Compilation edited by Claudia M. Lee copyright © 2002 Groundwood Books
Illustrations copyright © 2002 Rafael Yockteng

All rights reserved. No part of this book may be reproduced, stored in a retrieval system or transmitted in any form or by any means, without the prior written permission of the publisher or, in the case of photocopying or other reprographic copying, a licence from CANCOPY (Canadian Reprography Collective), Toronto, Ontario.

Groundwood Books / Douglas & McIntyre
720 Bathurst Street, Suite 500, Toronto, Ontario M5S 2R4

Distributed in the USA by Publishers Group West
1700 Fourth Street, Berkeley, CA 94710

National Library of Canada Cataloguing in Publication Data
Messengers of rain and other poems from Latin America
Translation of: Los mandaderos de la lluvia y otros poemas de America Latina
ISBN 0-88899-470-2
Children's poetry, Spanish. 2. Spanish poetry—21st century.
I. Lee, Claudia M. II. Yockteng, Rafael III. Leone, Andrew C.
PN6109.97.M3613 2002   j861'.708'09282   C2002-900523-X

Library of Congress Control Number: 2002102923

There are a few poems whose copyright owners have not been located despite diligent inquiry. The publishers would be grateful for information enabling them to make suitable acknowledgments in future printings.

Book design by Michael Solomon
Printed and bound in China by Everbest Printing Co. Ltd.

Table of Contents

✺

INTRODUCTION 6

Traditional Songs and Cooings
TRANSLATIONS BY Beatriz Zeller
9

*The cricket sings in the mountain
the tortoise in the sea,
they have sung for many years,
how much longer will they sing?*
TRANSLATIONS BY Sue Oringel
29

Magic Recipes
TRANSLATIONS BY David Unger
43

*Words and books
we can build
sand castles
and towers of salt*
TRANSLATIONS BY Andrew C. Leone
55

ABOUT THE POETS 76
INDEX OF POETS 79
INDEX OF TITLES 80

Introduction

THE CULTURES of Latin America are united by the heritage of the Castilian language, even though it is not a language common to all. We share a wide-ranging geography of mountains, valleys, rivers, deserts, jungles, cities, seas and plains that have also shaped us. Our poetry, like a quilt, is stitched together by the voices of native poets who speak of nature and animals, and poets who tell stories about people of many colors who inhabit new and old cities and who cross the bridges that separate and unite them. The words of our poets reveal a desire to understand life and a quest for peace that has eluded us for more than five centuries.

This anthology is dedicated to young people and all those who have adventurous spirits and the desire to make things better. Word by word, poets evoke a dawn, a silence or a dream universe. They recall a moment, share a feeling or tell a story, and with each word they teach the young and spark their aspirations. I hope that young people, with their natural eagerness to see and appreciate the world, find in these poems echos of the magical moments in the universe and the inspiration to dream their own.

This selection includes poems from nineteen Latin American countries. It is a small sample of the twentieth century and represents classic poets from our culture, as well as some lesser-known voices of women and men who write with refreshing and inspiring vitality.

Finding the poems was sometimes challenging, especially those by women and indigenous authors who were less widely published, but selecting the poems themselves was an easy task. Given that the anthology is dedicated to young readers, I sought out poems written in simple and direct language. I also wanted to share thoughts and feelings from our cultures. Themes such as magic and humor began to emerge from the poems, exhibiting a way of seeing life and solving problems, big and small. As my mother would say, "We have an innate ability to turn tragedy into comedy." With no intention of illustrating any particular point of view or political inclination, this collection reflects our struggle for liberty and justice, as well as the tradition of respect for and contemplation of nature. Finally, some poems show the complexity of the indigenous cultures in Latin America; others come from the songs and playground chants that belong to our oral tradition.

Claudia M. Lee
Philadelphia, March 2002

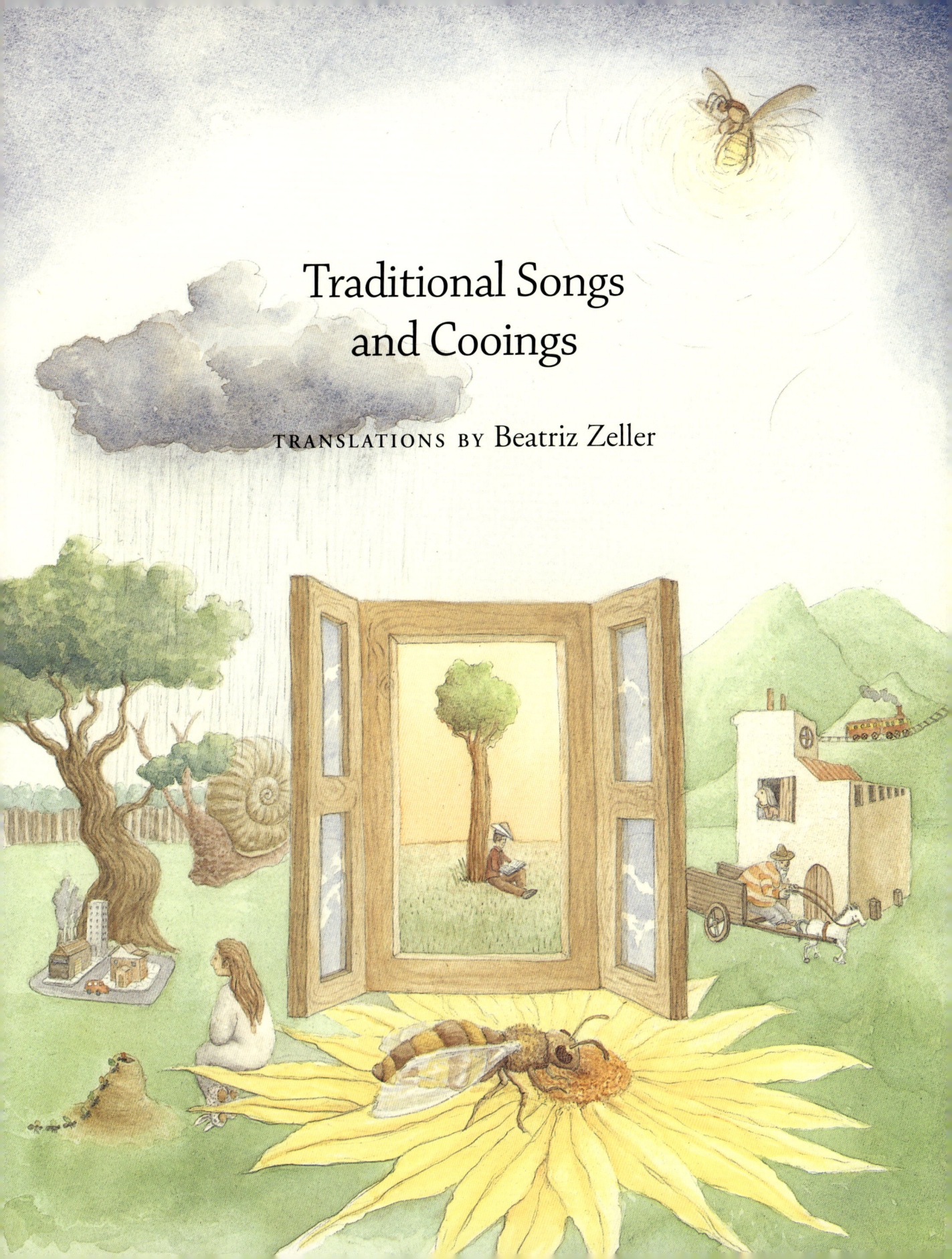

Traditional Songs
and Cooings

TRANSLATIONS BY Beatriz Zeller

RICE PUDDING
Traditional
BRAZIL AND LATIN AMERICA

Rice pudding is sweet,
but my greatest wish is
to marry the girl
who will steal my heart.

She will be a good reader,
she will spell the words right,
she will open the gates
for all to go out and play.

Will it be this one?
Will it be that one?
I choose this one for
she has stolen my heart.

Brincadeiras Cantadas. Editora Kuarup, Brazil, 1973.

SONG
Teresa Crespo de Salvador
ECUADOR
To my daughter María Isabel

Little pink shell,
sea flower,
my little girl wants
your song for herself.

Little blond bee,
you who makes magic with honey,
my little girl wants
to learn to swing as you do.

Dark little one of the moon,
grasshopper friend,
my little girl wants
to share your sweets.

Firefly, gentle sister
of the streetlamp,
my little girl wants to sleep now,
please put out your sun.

Hummingbird sweet,
shoot of the bamboo reed,
my little girl is now asleep.
Watch over her dreams.

Escuela y poesía. Cooperativa Editorial Magisterio, Colombia, 1997.

GIVE ME YOUR HAND
Gabriela Mistral
CHILE

Give me your hand so we may dance together
give me your hand so you will love me

We will be like a single flower
a single flower, that's all...

We will sing the same song,
we will dance to the same beat.
We will sway like a wheat sheaf
a wheat sheaf, that's all...

Your name is Rose, my name is Hope:
but your name you will forget,
as we become one with the dance
high up on the hill, that's all...

Lectura y comunicación. Santillana, Puerto Rico, 1997.

CHIEF KORUINKA'S SONG
Araucano traditional
CHILE

The entire earth is one soul
to which we belong.
Our souls will not die.
Change they might,
go out they will not.
We are one soul,
there is just one world.

Poesía indígena de América. Arango Editores, Colombia, 1995.

TROPIC
Rubén Darío
NICARAGUA

Such a fresh and cheerful morning!
The air grabs me by my nose,
the dogs bark, a boy shouts
a girl — round and pretty —
grinds her corn on the stone.

The farm hand walks down the path
carrying his tools, his knapsack,
while another in sandals and without a hat
looks for a cow with her calf
to milk next in the yard.

Smiling occasionally at the girl,
moving from stone to fire,
a handsome peasant boy
is on his knees sharpening
an ax on the rock where the river flows.

The light hides among the hills
under clear endless skies.
In the distance the cattle feeds
on grass that is thick and green,
crimson and gold beetles wander.

Under the bright sun and sounding
his horn, the cowboy approaches.
The cows and a white bull go by
their skin spotted with golden light
playing on the ropes around their necks.

The lady of the house stirs and stirs,
she dreams of a large
cup of hot chocolate
to pour down her throat
as she nibbles her buttered toast.

Biblioteca Virtual *Miguel de Cervantes,* 2000.

MORNING PRAYER TO THE CREATOR
Guaraní traditional
PARAGUAY

O, true Father, Ñamandú, the First!
On this your earth, Ñamandú, great heart,
the sun rises reflecting your great wisdom.
Because you ordered us, because you
gave us bow and arrow, made us rise,
we rose, walked tall once again.
Because of this, indestructible word,
word that can never be weakened,
we, a handful of paradise's orphans,
we repeat the word when we rise.
For this reason, may we be allowed
to rise many times.
O, true Father, Ñamandú, the First!

Poesía indígena de América. Arango Editores, Colombia, 1995.

SUMMER
Juana de Ibarbourou
URUGUAY

Song of the water, song of the river
endless song, deep-sounding song,
the forest above is dark,
the sands below are gold.

Song of the meadowlark
hidden in the cottonwood trees,
song of the wind among the branches
that bloom in the valley.

Song of the bees
inside the full treasure
of the beehive.
Song of the young baker girl
who comes to the river to wash clothes.
And song, song, song
of my soul drunk and mad
with summer's light!

Poemas escogidos para niños. Editorial Piedra Santa, Guatemala, 1998.

LITTLE MOON, LOOK, RUN OVER HERE, COME
Enrique Solano Rodríguez
PERU

Little moon, look, run over here, tell
the stars your daughters
that my little girl is crying:
she wants to go out
to play with them.

Little moon, look, run over here, come
with your daughters, hide those tears
for my little girl is crying to play
    round-around.

Virtual page of Lambayeque's poetry, 2000.
By permission of the author.

GIRL STORIES
Carolina Escobar Sarti
GUATEMALA

She's just been born
among winter and lace.

She was born short
of wings
and flights.

She was given dolls,
rings, flowers,
soft dresses.

Stories about princes,
about fairies she was told,
dreams were dreamt for her.

She was taught set recipes,
things were hidden from her,
they taught her to walk
the narrowest roads.

The prince arrived
on a black horse,
took her to the castle
of his grandparents.

The little girl began to die
among autumn and dreams.

The years passed
without pain
without mystery.

And the ripped ruffles
left everything
exposed:
no dreams remained,
no prince, no fire,
just endless weariness and silence.

That's when the other baby was born,
a girl born of spring.

She was born big
with desires
and dreams.

She was granted wings, words,
stars
and kisses.

Everyone listened to her tales
of adventure and play.
They rejoiced in her poetry.

They taught her to sing
to feel,
she flew in the air
barely touching the ground.

She did not wait for her prince,
but took flight instead,
lived on the sea, on the earth
and in the sky.

La penúltima luz. Editorial del pensativo,
Guatemala, 1999.

TALE OF THE WANDERING TADPOLE
Rafael Pombo
COLOMBIA

Tadpole Rinrín, Lady Toad's son,
went out this morning, tall and handsome,
wearing stylish shorts and a fashionable tie,
beribboned hat and the perfect waistcoat.
"Don't you go out!" his mother warned,
but with a wave of his hand he stepped out of the house.

On his way down the street he ran into Mouse,
his neighbor, and he said, "Come with me my friend,
we'll go for a visit to old Mrs. Mouse.
She'll have a fine spread, much to dine on."

In no time they were there. Mouse went ahead,
and stretching his neck grabbed onto the door knocker:
Two, three knocks he gave. "Who is it?" asked a small voice.
"It's me, Mrs. Mouse, came to say hello."

"Are you in?" "Yes sir, I am here;
happy to see the two of you today.
I was working at what I do best, spinning
cotton, but no matter, please do come in."

They greeted each, together shook hands all three.
Said Mr. Rodent, being the more experienced,
"My good friend, the one here in green, is feeling hot.
Please serve him some beer, will you not?"

And while the scoundrel downed that cool glass,
he sent for a guitar, let the party begin!
The lady asked Tadpole to sing her a tune,
a nice little song to help her along.

"I'd love to oblige, madam,
but can't right at this time of day
as my throat is dry, as dry as hay
and these new clothes are too tight for my voice."

"So sorry to hear that," answered Mrs. Mouse.
Why don't you loosen that tie, unbutton your vest,
and I'll sing you this little song
with meaning and love."

While the performance was going on,
song and drink and orchestral tones,
in waltzed Lady Cat and her cats through the door
and turned that scene into a day of judgment.

Old Mrs. Cat pulled Mousie hard by
the ear, meowing her greetings, moving along
while her cat children seized old Mrs. Mouse,
now by the tail, now by the paws.

Observing the show-down old Mr. Tadpole
grabbed his hat, took a huge leap
and opened the door, with both hand and nose,
bidding everyone present a joyous good-night.

He went on leaping so high and so fast
that he lost hold of his hat, got his shirt stuck
right inside the beak of a voracious duck,
who swallowed him whole down his huge throat.

Before one could count one, two, three,
all was concluded. Mr. Mouse and Mrs. Mouse
and also the toad were quickly consumed by numerous cats. Duck finished his dinner
and poor Lady Toad was left all alone!

País de versos. Tres Culturas Editores, Colombia, 1999.

TOMORROW SUNDAY
Germán Berdiales
ARGENTINA

Tomorrow Sunday
there will be a wedding
between peacock
and white dove.
Her godparents
will be her mother dovetail
and old Mr. Duck, quack, quack.

The father of the groom
will stand in as his godfather
and the gray heron
will be his godmother.
The bride's dress will have a train,
the groom will wear a morning coat.
Standing tall
they will walk down the aisle.
A brilliant wedding party
will follow the newlyweds.
The best of the best
will be on hand for the marriage.
In couples will come
a lark with her robin,
a distinguished turkey
with a ring dove
and a swallow walking
ladylike by her cardinal.

From the branch that will
stand as the altar,
a red-chested warbler
will bless everyone.

Poemas escogidos. Editorial Piedra Santa, Guatemala, 1998.

THE KITE
Claudia Lars
EL SALVADOR

Tall flower among the clouds
— the best part of the summer —
its long stem of song
planted in my palm.

A gift of spring
renewed every year
to dress up the day
and play while it stays.

Unfurled flag of the party
escaping in mid flight...
tambourine shaken
by distant whirlwinds.

Little fish in the air
intent on leaping.
Bird tangled
in its own tail of cloth.

Midday moon,
its face like a clown's
Lord of the balancing act.
Dancers of the sky.

The child invents these wings
and knots them to his arms...
Messenger from the blue.
Heart of summer.

Poemas escogidos. Editorial Piedra Santa, Guatemala, 1998.

THE TRAVELER
Humberto Ak'abal
GUATEMALA

I walked all through the night
searching for my shadow.

— It had become entangled
with the darkness.

Utiwww
cried the coyote.

I kept walking.

Tu tu tukuuur…
tooted the owl.

I just kept on walking.

Zotz' zotz' zotz'…
went the bat while biting
the ear of an unknowing gnat.

Then it was daybreak.

My shadow was so long
that it covered the whole road.

Guardián de la caída de agua. Artemis Edinter, Guatemala, 2000. By permission of the author.

JOSÉ MANUEL
Ismael Lee Vallejo
COLOMBIA

Little rag-clown. My pal,
My only friend in childhood.
Little rag-clown, you take
the cold baths and scoldings so well.
Those that I give you for no reason.
You watch over me while I sleep.
If I jump you jump, you laugh with me,
you're loyal and cry when they scold me.
José Manuel my little clown.
One day when I grow up,
I will miss you in my sadness.
My sweet friend, my pal,
little clown, José Manuel.

By permission of the author.

THE TUKUMUX BIRD
Humberto Ak'abal
GUATEMALA

The Tukumux bird was singing
rocking to and fro on the shores of the river.

A girl came by and tried to grab him
to take him on home.

But the bird wouldn't let her
and started to dance instead.

Without realizing it
she started to dance along.

They danced, they danced and they danced
until daylight was gone.

The Tukumux bird got entangled with the night
    and the girl woke up, crying.

Desnuda como la primera vez, Artemis Edinter, Guatemala, 2000. By permission of the author.

ICNOCUICATL
Fragment of a Náhuatl traditional
MEXICO

What will my heart do?
In vain we have come,
sprouted from the earth.
Is this the way? Am I
to go, leave, like flowers once wilted?
Will nothing be left of my name?
Will nothing be left of my fame on this earth?
At least the flowers! At least the songs!

Thus spoke Tochihuitzin,
and also Coyolchuihqui:
"We don't come here to live,
we come here only to dream,
we come here only to be
like spring."
Our life sprouts,
it blooms, it wilts.
That is all.
Thus spoke Coyolchuihqui,
this was said by Tochihuitzin.

Poesía indígena de América. Arango Editores, Colombia, 1995.

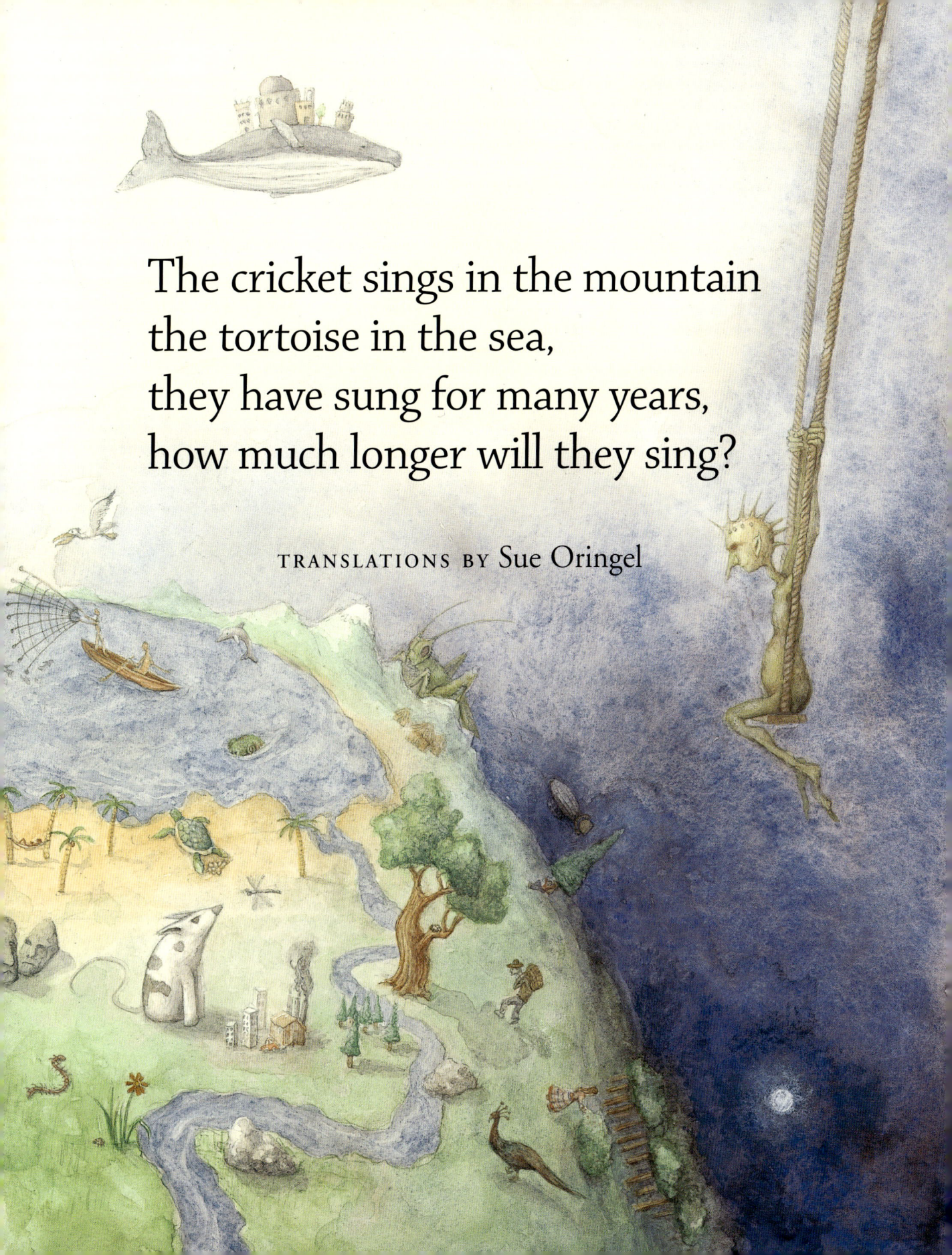

The cricket sings in the mountain
the tortoise in the sea,
they have sung for many years,
how much longer will they sing?

TRANSLATIONS BY Sue Oringel

FROM WHERE THE ROSE?
Esther María Ossés
PANAMA

— Black is the seed,
the landscape dark,
colorless, the water
that bathes it all.

From where comes the rose,
the bright crimson rose?
From where that red,
a little black seed?

— A bit of moon,
of sun and of wind.
A bit of rain.
        The rest... secret.

Escuela y poesía. Cooperativa Editorial Magisterio, Colombia, 1997.

LADY SPRING
Gabriela Mistral
CHILE

Lady Spring
wears only what's exquisite,
dresses in a lemon tree
and flowering orange.

Takes for her sandals
several roomy leaves,
and for earrings —
a few red fuchsias.

Go out to meet her
walking those roads.
Sunup to sundown
she goes crazy warbling.

Lady Spring,
she of fecund breath,
laughs at all
the pains of the earth.

She doesn't believe the one talking
of stingy, vicious lives.
How can she find them
among the jasmines?

How can she find them
next to the fountains
of gilded mirrors
and radiant fields?

From the ailing soil
of cloudy brown cracks,
rose bushes kindle
their red pirouettes.

She places her laces,
clasps her green things
on the sorrowful stone
of the ancient graves...

Lady Spring,
with your glorious hands
make us scatter
roses all our lives.

Roses of joy,
roses of pardon,
roses of caresses —
and exultation.

Gabriela Mistral y los niños. Editorial Everest, S.A. Spain, 1988.

THE RIDER
Aramís Quintero
CUBA

There, within the deep fields
quietly draped in calm
the shadow of a palm
meets a crossing white horse.

Quietly on horseback
it moves toward the distance.
There toward the depth
of the fields in silence.

And over it all
dusk like a song falls.
And that white horse
is now turning red.

Días de aire. Editorial Gente Nueva,
Cuba, 1982. By permission of the author.

IN THE GARDEN
Emilia Gallego Alfonso
CUBA

Platero, silvery fast-walking donkey,
searching for butterflies,
trotting into the garden.

Platero, silvery fast-walking donkey,
you found wings and roses
yellow and crimson.

Trotting among the rose bushes
and butterfly wings went Platero,
fast-walking donkey who rushes.

Para un niño travieso. Universidad de La Habana, Cuba, 1981. By permission of the author.

THE SQUIRREL
Amado Nervo
MEXICO

The squirrel runs,
the squirrel flies,
the squirrel jumps
in graceful style.

— Mama, doesn't the squirrel
go to school?

Come, little squirrel:
I have a cage
that is very graceful.

No, I prefer
my tree trunk
and my burrow.

Poemas escogidos para niños. Editorial Piedra Santa, Guatemala, 1998.

MOTHER WHALE
Natives from the island of Tiburón
MEXICO

The mother whale is
satisfied.
Swims on the surface, very
fast.
There are no sharks near
but she swims and swims, always
quickly,
many leagues that way,
comes back this way.
Later she sinks to the very
bottom
and four baby whales are born.

Poesía indígena de América. Arango Editores, Colombia, 1995.

THE LITTLE TORTOISE
Manuel Felipe Rugeles
VENEZUELA

The little tortoise
leaves the river
to find sunshine.
She is shivering.

The little tortoise
isn't ashamed,
and she has fallen asleep
alone in the sand.

The little tortoise
loses all sense.
Now she doesn't remember
where she was born.

They have taken her
from San Fernando,
and she doesn't know
how or when.

Now in an aquarium
of algae and flowers,
they've painted her
a million colors!

Antología de poesia infantil venezolana. Fe y alegría, Venezuela, 1983.

THE COYOLARES (PALM TREES)
Froilán Turcios
HONDURAS

In the fertile forests of Olancho,
combed by soft sonorous winds,
in the barrenness of summers, the palms
show off their branches of gold.

Bristling with radiant spines,
fronds unfurl to the sun their greens,
shedding in evening hours
light rains of fragrant flowers.

The man with his vibrating ax
hurls the tree to plain earth,
stripping its useless branches,
and in the tree his dagger opens a hole
and the delicious liquor that enfolds it
with sweet fire intoxicates his heart.

Poemas escogidos para niños. Editorial Piedra Santa, Guatemala, 1998.

MESSENGERS OF THE RAIN
Humberto Ak'abal
GUATEMALA

The song of the cenzontles
announces that the rain
is coming down the road.

The fireflies
with their dance of yellow lights
say that the rain is near.

And when the toads
undress their rock,
dark clouds erase the heavens,
and the first drops
of rain begin to fall.

Desnuda como la primera vez. Artemis Edinter,
Guatemala, 2000. By permission of the author.

RESURRECTION
Julia Esquivel
GUATEMALA

I love life —
the sun, the howl of the wind in the mountain,
the tempests, the thunder,
the happy song of the birds,
the happiness of rabbits,
the barking of dogs
and the stroll of the snails
after the rain.

I love life —
the rebel gypsy's deep song,
the ancestral lament of the flute,
the violent dance of the Russians
and the timid smiles of Native children.

I love life
skin dark or light, the shine on the cheeks of
    Black people,
tresses the color
of corn silk.
I love the never-idle ants, the lowing of cows
and the tinkling of their bells
in the Alps.

I love life —
the buzzing of gluttonous bees,
the mischief of the squirrels,
the marvelous fur of the fox,
the pretty paces of the fawn
and the horse's gallantry
with its mane in the wind.

The Certainty of the Spring. Epica, Guatemala, 1993. By permission of the author.

THE NEST
Alfredo Espino
EL SALVADOR

It's because a mountain bird has made
its morning nest in the hollow of a tree
that the tree wakes up with music in its breast,
as if it had a musical heart inside.

If the sweet little bird peeps out the hole
to drink dew, to drink perfume,
the mountain tree gives me the feeling
    that its heart has left it, singing.

Poemas escogidos para niños. Editorial Piedra Santa, Guatemala, 1998.

THE FROG AND THE MOON
Javier Villegas Fernández
PERU

A frog croaked
camouflaged in the water,
and the moon traveled
dressed in petticoats.

The enchanted frog
leaped and leaped,
and the moon looked on
with a silverplated glow.

The frog and the moon
went looking for each other,
and close to the lagoon
they were chatting.

Together they planned
their voyage of night,
and both went away
at the very same time.

But behind the moon
the frog was rowing,
because in the lagoon
the moon was going.

Poroporo. Revista de Literatura Infantil y Promoción de la Lectura, Peru, 2000. By permission of the author.

FUCHSIAS
Óscar Alfaro
BOLIVIA

The caramel-colored girls
are dancing in the air.

With skirts of stars they scatter
the afternoon with sparks.

Oh, how they go dancing down
the musical scales of notes!

With golden slippers,
with blood-colored fans.

Above the dewy moons
they step and whirl and fall.

And they hang from the whiskers
of my valley's old sun.

Escuela y poesía. Cooperativa Editorial Magisterio, Colombia, 1997.

WE WILL GO TO THE MOUNTAIN
Alfonsina Storni
ARGENTINA

To the mountain
now we'll go,
to the mountain
to play.
On the slopes
the tree grows,
the brook shines,
the flower sways.
How lovely the air,
how beautiful the sun,
blue is heaven,
one feels close to God.
Long live my valleys,
the Calchaquies.
The afternoon is made
of velvet,
mallows in the
rocks,
rose in the heavens.
To the mountain
let's form a round,
a round of children,
a circular round.

Lectura y comunicación. Santillana, Puerto Rico, 1997.

MAYO
Maya Cu
GUATEMALA

There will be something
in each pine
for my dreams

    There will be moss
in each space
of my veins

    There will be flowers
    in each thorn
    of hope

There will be
  a song
    in each step
      of soul

There will be my
  swollen world
  in each one
  of these
      — these that are
  of them

        — those that live

Novísimos. Editorial Cultura, Guatemala, 1996.
By permission of the author.

THIS SAID CHIRAS THE CHICKEN
Víctor Eduardo Caro
COLOMBIA

This said Chiras the Chicken
when they were going to kill him:
"Strike me quickly, my madam,
put the water to warm.

Throw a coal in the stove
and don't stop blowing
so the day doesn't catch us
and the master is coming for lunch.

But listen to me dear madam
I beg you one little thing:
don't twist my neck
like that woman, Trinidad.

There are a million kinder ways
to put an animal to sleep
and to make its sleep last
for all eternity.

Please, good madam, comply
with my final wish
and dispatch me very promptly
without pain or cruelty."

The madam was a lady
of extreme charity;
she remained quite confused
at what had been said.

She studied the matter deeply,
consulted authorities,
read various volumes
in English and German;

Bought ingredients, flasks,
a thermometer, a compass,
two hypodermic syringes
and I don't know what else.

And in tests and experiments
in little crystal tubes,
in readings and conferring
her time flies by.

Meanwhile Chiras the Chicken
sings happily in the yard,
"Strike me quickly, my madam.
put the water to warm!"

País de versos. Tres Culturas Editores, Colombia, 1995.

Magic Recipes

TRANSLATIONS BY
David Unger

THE LITTLE WEAVING SPIDER
Emilia Gallego Alfonso
CUBA

There's a spider in my courtyard
who works without rest day and night;
among the flowers and the branches,
weaving cloth of glass and light.

And on the threads of its fabric
the sun reflects more rays
than in the fountain waters
where the sunflowers dance away.

Para un niño travieso. Universidad de La Habana, Cuba, 1981. By permission of the author.

SIGN OF THE GERANIUM I
Otto Raúl González
GUATEMALA

The peddler went sadly and quietly by
under the rain that erased
his footsteps in the night;
and he had a geranium in his chest.

The worker trudged alone, gazing down,
sweating,
his soul and his shoes fraying;
and he had a geranium in his eyes.

A blue ship of vowels,
The new young school teacher
sailed by, and she had a geranium in her
braids.

Voz y voto del geranio. Editorial Cultura, Guatemala, 1994.

SIGN OF THE GERANIUM II
Otto Raúl González
GUATEMALA

The nimble young woman went by,
a gondola filled with such sweetness,
the most beautiful girl in town,
the maid who worked in a mansion;
and she had a geranium in her belly.

The most downtrodden man went by,
that short, barefoot crier
who delivers the day's news to the town,
he who sometimes goes to school
and whose eyes are always burning
with cold, hunger and sleep;
and he had a geranium in his cheeks.

They all had a geranium,
but instead of the sign of the cross
they practiced the sign of the geranium.

Voz y voto del geranio. Editorial Cultura, Guatemala, 1994.

INDIAN CANOES
Aramís Quintero
CUBA

Everything you say
is heard by a rabbit.

Can't you see his long ears?

Whether he is near
or far away.

Can't you see his long ears?

They snare everything
that you say.

Indian canoes.

Virtual magazine *Cuatrogatos,* 2000.
By permission of the author.

CASTLES
Excilia Saldaña
CUBA

There's a castle
in the sky,
there's a castle
in the sea.
The sky castle is made of wings,
the sea castle of water and waves.

There's a castle
in the mountain pines,
there's a castle
in the sea.
The pine castle is full of birdsong,
the sea castle of sand.

There's a castle
in my blood,
there's a castle
in the sea.
The blood castle is my child:
sky, wings, birdsong and sea.

Virtual magazine *Cuatrogatos,* 2000.

MAGIC POTION FOR ALL KINDS OF USES
Irene Vasco
COLOMBIA

Toss into a large pot
two tomatoes, either whole or chopped,
two pieces of junk, three kilos of salt
and one of glass,
a dash of fog and a sprinkle of pepper,
two cups of ivy and a kilo of stone.

Beat all the ingredients, add another tomato,
if it needs more salt, wait till the end,
if it tastes bad, add thunder
and if it's okay, add a twisting pinch.

Don't cook or bake it.
At any time, at any place,
drink just a drop
and the rest…
simply throw the slop away.

Escuela y poesía. Cooperativa Editorial Magisterio, Colombia, 1997.
By permission of the author.

THE WALL
Nicolás Guillén
CUBA

To build this wall,
bring me each and every hand:
black hands,
white hands.
Yes,
a wall running
from the seashore to the mountains,
from the mountains to the seashore,
over there, on the horizon.
"Knock, knock!"
"Who's there?"
"A rose and a carnation…"
"Open the gate!"
"Knock, knock!"
"Who's there?"
"A colonel's saber."
"Close the gate!"
"Knock, knock!"
"Who's there?"
"The dove and the laurel leaf…"
"Open the gate!"
"Knock, knock!"
"Who's there?"
"The scorpion and the centipede…"
"Close the gate!"

The gate opens
to a friend's heart;
the gate closes
to poison and knives;
the gate opens
to the myrtle tree and the mint;
the gate closes
to a rattling snake;
the gate opens
to the nightingale in a flower...

Let's build a wall
With everyone's hands:
black hands,
white hands.
A wall running
from the seashore to the mountains,
from the mountains to the seashore,
over there, on the horizon…

Lectura y comunicación. Ediciones Santillana, Puerto Rico, 1997.

WITH THE SUN AND THE MOON
Marcos Leibovich
ARGENTINA

The moon is a harp:
the sun, a trombone.
With sun and moon
I'll compose my tune.

The moon is made of flour,
the sun of honey.
With moon and sun,
what a delicious cake!

The moon is a lily;
the sun, a tulip.
With sun and moon,
a thousand bouquets are made.

The moon is stillness;
the sun, motion.
With sun and moon,
what a great lesson!

Lectura y comunicación. Ediciones Santillana, Puerto Rico, 1997.

THE SEA SHELL
Emilia Gallego Alfonso
CUBA

The sea shell on the shore
holds the clear
and rapid laughter
of the waves as they crash.

The sea shell on the shore
holds the short
and simple grief
of the waves as they leave.

Echo of clear laughter
and of simple grief:
sea shell on the beach,
sea shell on the shore.

Y dice una mariposa. Editorial Gente Nueva, Cuba, 1983. By permission of the author.

THE MAGICIAN
David Chericián
CUBA

A very magical magician
went out the door
and his hat flew back
through the same door;
he returned, crossed his legs
and sat at the table.

A cat comes out of the hat,
an airplane out of the cat,
a handkerchief out of the airplane,
a sun out of the handkerchief,
a wide river out of the sun,
a flower out of the river,
music comes out of the flower,
and out of the flower, I come.

Virtual magazine *Cuatrogatos*, 2000.
By permission of the author.

FIREFLY
Aramís Quintero
CUBA

In the night full
of stars and lights,
a tiny star flies alone,
blinking in silence.

Little voice flying by,
tell us a story.
We hear nothing. A thought
seems to be flying by.

Escuela y poesía. Cooperativa Editorial Magisterio, Colombia, 1997. By permission of the author.

WATERCOLOR
Clarisa Ruiz
COLOMBIA

Trapped inside
The watercolor case,
The sky, the sun,
Trees,
Roses,
The way home,
The cloud that comes and goes,
The rainbow.

Virtual magazine *Cuatrogatos*, 2000.
By permission of the author.

RAIN
Humberto Ak'abal
GUATEMALA

Little threads of water
seep out of the clouds
and fill up with earth.

Such fresh green fields!

The rain frolics
splashing around in the mud.

The earth smells.

And the birds
let their songs fly off.

By permission of the author.

THE LITTLE BOAT
Humberto Ak'abal
GUATEMALA

The afternoon didn't want to end
It was all water, water and more water.

— The little boy laughed —
He let go of the sailboat
The wind sprang from his mouth
And the boat sailed away.

The little boy watched
The boat sail on and on
And he was inside the boat,
Dreaming, singing,
Until it sank.

A new page from his notebook
And his voyage continued
Inside another little paper boat.

By permission of the author.

Words and books we can build sand castles and towers of salt

TRANSLATIONS BY Andrew C. Leone

AT THE WATER'S EDGE
Octavio Paz
MEXICO

The tiny ant walking
at the water's edge
      seems to say
goodbye when bending her antennae

I can't help thinking of you as I look at her
So self assured in her mission
      so beautiful

Always almost drowning
and always somehow surviving

Always saying goodbye
to those who won't see her again.

Octavio Paz. *Obra poética, 1935-1988*, Seix Barral, México, 2000.

EXAMPLE
Octavio Paz
MEXICO

The butterfly flew about the cars.
Marie José told me: it must be Chuang Tzu
passing through New York.
                          But the butterfly
didn't know she was a butterfly
with dreams of being Chuang Tzu
                    or Chuang Tzu
with dreams of being a butterfly.
The butterfly never doubted:
                    it flew.

Octavio Paz. *Obra poética, 1935-1988*, Seix Barral, México, 2000.

THE SUN HAS NO POCKETS
María Elena Walsh
ARGENTINA

The sun has no pockets,
the moon has no sea.
In a world so big
why so little space?

I have seen square-looking flowers
and a military bird.
In a world so big
why so little space?

Why must we pay to breathe
air that belongs to us all.
In a world so big
why so little space?

> *And where do I go*
> *and where do you go*
> *and what will be of us*
> *whirling inside a bubble*
in search
of humanity.

Las canciones. Seix Barral, Argentina, 1994.
By permission of the author.

THE KEY
Humberto Ak'abal
GUATEMALA

The key was always in her possession;
that was her habit.

And grandma Saq'kil,
some days before leaving us,
squeezed a key
in her hand.

What did she keep in her chest?

The last day
her hand relaxed
and she let it fall.

From the chest flew
a golden butterfly.

Desnuda como la primera vez. Artemis Edinter,
Guatemala, 2000. By permission of the author.

BLACK MAN FROM PANAMA
Carlos F. Changmarín
PANAMA

I am a black man from Marañón
black man from Guachapalí,
born black as you see me,
in a corner dark as coal.

I am the tiger and the lion
I'm the hardwood-swinging club,
I'm the early morning star
I'm the sparkling diamond stone...
I come with a freedom song,
and a people's sovereignty.

I am the son of a black woman
and a black man from San Miguel,
He was black just like his father
black was his mother as well.

Black I stood as black I was,
black I stay and black I grow,
black I fight until death takes me;
till she bids me come along.

Black I came across the sea
in the dim colonial night,
black as none and blacker still
as I dug through the canal.

I don't moan, I don't cry,
you will not hear me complain,
even as I leave a black man
to this world, it's how I came.

Some black men indeed are black:
black as was the Cuban clobber;
the black man who cut the chains,
our hero black Bayano.

I am Black from living blackness,
black are my drum and my rhythm,
black my Cumbia and Curacha
black my dreams and my love.

And being black shall be no reason
to suffer someone else's abuse...
A day will come, it will be soon.
Hear my shout, "Slave? I refuse!"

Crimson blood, people you'll see
floating wide from sea to sea
and that day black conga players
will rise to their feet and dance.

I am a black man from Marañón
Black man from Guachapalí.
O, black woman touch me here
where my heart beats on!
Let's dance this *son*.
Come around, make a half circle
and let me say clearly
singing as I do,
I'd rather die fighting
while I hear sweet freedom's ruse.

Poesía Testimonial Latinoamericana. Editores Mexicanos Unidos, Mexico, 1999.

LAND OF MY BIRTH
Julio Herrera y Reissig
URUGUAY

O land, dear land of my birth,
so many pleasures I owe thee!
You remind me of my loved ones
those dearest to me;
you remind me of my youth
and its innocent child's play;
you remind me of the days
of greatest fortune and peace,
my mother's hand's soft touch
and my grandfather's stories.

O land, dear land of my birth,
so many pleasures I owe thee!

Poemas escogidos para niños. Editorial Piedra Santa, Guatemala, 1998.

QUESTIONS AROUND TEA TIME
Nicanor Parra
CHILE

This pale-looking man seems
like a figure in a wax museum;
Looks through torn lace curtains.
What is worth more, riches or beauty?
What is worth more, a moving stream
or the grass glued to the shore?
Far away a bell tolls
opening or closing another wound.
What is more real, the water in a pool
or the girl gazing at her reflection in it?
Who knows, people insist
on building sandcastles.
What is the greater treasure, the transparent glass
or the hand of the man who made it?
The air we breathe is heavy
with ashes, smoke and sadness:
What has been seen once, cannot appear
the same again, whirlwind of dead leaves.
It's time for tea, toast, margarine,
all wrapped in some kind of mist.

The Antipoetry of Nicanor Parra. New York University Press, USA, 1975.

MORNING ROUTINE
Rubén Darío (from Songs of Life and Hope)
NICARAGUA

Clear morning hours
when a thousand golden trumpets
cry to the divine daylight!
Hail the brightness of the majestic Sun!

    Anguished as we are in our ignorance
of what's to come, let us greet
the fragrance filled vessel
urged on by ivory oars.

    Whether Epicurean or dreamers
let us love this glorious Life,
always wearing flower garlands
always bearing torch alight!

    Let us squeeze from the bunches
of our transitory life
the pleasures for which we live
and the glorious sparkling wine.

    Let us spin the yarn of Love,
let us do good for its own sake
and then sleep as would the just
forever and ever. Amen.

Biblioteca virtual *Miguel de Cervantes,* 2000.

A SEA WALL
Julia de Burgos
PUERTO RICO

I'll make a sea wall
with my bit of happiness…
I don't want the sea to know
that my heart harbors great sorrow.

I don't want the sea to know
the shore this side of my land…
I have no dreams left
desperate for shade in the sand.

I don't want the sea to notice
the blue of mourning on my path…
(My eyelids were sunrises
till the tempest blew past!)

I don't want the sea to cry
new storms at my door…
All the eyes of the wind
saw me dead for evermore.

I'll make a sea wall
with my bit of happiness,
tiny happiness of knowing
it's my hand that stops it.

I don't want the sea to reach
the thirst of my poem,
blind in the midst of light,
broken in the midst of absence.

El mar y tú y otros poemas. Ediciones Huracán, Puerto Rico, 1981.

TO ACHIEVE PEACE
Roque Dalton
EL SALVADOR

When the moon says its farewell to the water
with its hidden current of inexpressive light

Then we shall steal the rifles,
hurriedly.

There's no need to fight the sentry, the wretch
is but the expression of a collective dream,
a uniform filled with sighs
mindful of the sowing.
Let's leave him, full of himself, to drink his moon and granite.

Our shadow thrown upon his eyelids will suffice
to make our point.

We shall steal all the rifles,
inexorably.

We'll have to carry them with care,
but without stopping
and abandon them amidst the explosions
upon the patio stones.

Beyond that, nothing but the wind remains.

We'll have all the guns,
overjoyed.

Never mind the momentary frost
cowering beneath the sweat of our fright,
nor the doubtful link of our breath
with the ample mist, plentiful in space:
we shall walk to the harvest fields
and hopeful we shall bury
all the rifles,
so that gun powder roots will explode their metal shoots
into butterflies
in an arrogant spring to come
filled with doves.

...*La ventana en el rostro*. UCA Editores, El Salvador, 1998.

THIS CHILD DON SIMÓN
Manuel Felipe Rugeles
VENEZUELA

The child Simón Bolivar
happily played the drum
in a yard of pomegranates
that were always in full bloom.

He later rode a horse.
They say the steed was fast;
through the fields of San Mateo,
among all horsemen he was best.

But one day he grew to greatness
he who had been the child Simón
and rode on upon his horse
with ease, while dreaming on.

From Angostura to Bolivia
he was a warrior and a winner,
through the plains and mountain paths,
under the rain and the sun.

On his horse he rides through history
this child Don Simón,
as he rode through the Americas
When he was Liberator.

Antología de poesia infantil venezolana. Fe y alegría, Venezuela, 1983.

WARTIME POSTCARD
María Elena Walsh
ARGENTINA

A silken paper leaf
floats in hazy smoke.
The current pushes on
a bridge now just a wreck.
Tears.

The evening bows,
gunpowder and fog.
The ashes fall like rain
silently.
Tears.

Oh, will they ever return
the flower to the branch
and the fragrance to baked bread.

Burnt trees,
pale and ragged.
Shipwrecked upon a rivulet
floats away a sandal.
Tears.

Ghost like steps
run off in pieces.
Shadowy and willowy.
A multitude of mothers.
Tears.

Oh, will they ever return
the flower to the branch
and the fragrance to baked bread.
Tears, tears, tears!

Las canciones. Seix Barral, Argentina, 1994. By permission of the author.

BOATS AND DREAMS
Francisco Feliciano Sánchez
PUERTO RICO

My little paper ship
wasn't built in a shipyard.
My little paper ship
is the fruit of my dreams.

Takes on a different life;
gullible it sails the world
helping people as it does
their dreams to hold.

One mustn't ever question
the whys of the imagination.
If you want to fly, fly!
If so dictates your heart.

Poemas para niñas y niños. Editorial Azogue,
Puerto Rico, 2000. By permission of the author.

RIVULET
Aramís Quintero
CUBA

Through the tender grass
of the green meadow,
among smooth stones
and golden stones,
with its ringing, singing, light laughter,
there goes the thread of water.
Rivulet.

It goes hurriedly,
important waters, it says,
are waiting for it
out at sea.

But a few steps from
its fountain spring,
it collects in a small pool —
the kind that dries
when there is no rain.

And the rivulet says
that the deep ocean awaits.
Fine with me if it says so
and if it believes so!

Un elefante en la cuerda floja. Ediciones Union,
Cuba, 1998. By permission of the author.

PLENTY
Miguel Ángel Asturias
GUATEMALA

To give is to love,
give plentifully,
for each drop of water
give back a torrent.

This is how we were made,
made to fling
seeds into the furrow
and stars into the sea
and woe be to him
who will not exhaust
Lord, his part
and on his return remark,
"Empty is my heart
as empty as a pouch!"

Poemas escogidos para niños. Editorial Piedra Santa, Guatemala, 1998.

THE LITTLE DANDELION
Carmen Lyra
COSTA RICA

I am the little
dandelion,
amidst the grass I seem
like a little sun.

I am shriveling,
I have shriveled,
I am losing my petals,
I have lost my petals.

Now I am a globe
fine and delicate,
now I am lace,
silvery lace.

We are the seeds
of the dandelion,
tiny little spiders
of the rarest beauty.

God's hands
put us together.
Here comes the wind:
Brothers, so long!

Escuela y Poesía. Cooperativa Editorial Magisterio, Colombia, 1997.

THE POOR LITTLE OLD LADY
Rafael Pombo
COLOMBIA

Once there lived an old lady
who had nothing left to eat
except for meat, fruit and sweets,
cakes, eggs, bread and fish.

She drank hot broth and chocolate,
milk, wine, tea and coffee,
but the poor lady could find
nothing at all to eat and drink.

And the poor little old lady
didn't even have a home
except of course for a mansion
with an orchard and a lawn.

No one ever cared for her
but for Andrés, Juan and Gil
and eight chambermaids, two pages
in their livery and frills.

She had nowhere to sit
but for chairs and ample sofas
with their ottomans and pillows
and plenty of soft cushions.

She had no bed except for one
more ornate than an altar
with a mattress of soft goose down
lots of silk and much fine linen.

And this poor little old lady
every year until the end
added one more year of aging
and had one less year to live.

And when gazing at her reflection
there was always to haunt her
another bespectacled old lady
with a bonnet and a wig.

Oh this poor little old lady
really had no clothes to wear
other than suits of many styles
and thousands of kinds of silks.

And were it not for her shoes,
sandals, boots and slippers too,
she would have to walk all barefoot
the poor wretch on the floor.

She never did feel hunger
after finishing her meal,
and she never was too healthy
when she wasn't feeling well.

Then she died ill with wrinkles,
curved she seemed a number three,
and she never again complained
not of hunger nor of thirst.

And this poor little old lady
when she died left nothing more
than gold, jewels, lands and houses
eight cats and one songbird.

May she rest in peace and God willing
that we too should have the fortune
to be as poor as this old thing
and die of her same afflictions.

Poemas encantados y canciones de cuna.
Panamericana Editorial, Colombia, 1999.

FAREWELL
Anonymous, attributed to Jorge Luis Borges

If I could live my life anew,
in the next I'd attempt more mistakes.
I wouldn't try to be so perfect,
I would relax more.
I'd be more foolish than I've been,
In fact I'd take very few things too seriously.
I'd be less sanitary.

I'd take more chances.
take more trips,
I'd contemplate more sunsets.
I'd climb more mountains, swim more rivers.
I'd go to more places,
and to the ones I've never been.
I'd eat more ice cream and fewer beans.
I'd have more real problems
and fewer imaginary ones.

I was one of those
who lived every minute of his life
sensibly and productively,
surely I had happy moments.
But if I could start anew
I would try to have only good moments.
And if you don't know it
that's what life is made of,
just moments,
don't miss out on the now.

I was one of those who
never went anywhere
without a thermometer,
a hot water bottle,
an umbrella and a parachute.

If I could live my life again,
I'd go naked until the end of autumn,
I'd ride more often in the little carriages,
I'd contemplate more daybreaks
and play more often with children.
If my life were again ahead of me...

But as you see, I am 85
and I know I am dying...

Luis. Salas.net, Virtual Page, 2001.

About the Poets

Humberto Ak'abal (1952-) Born in Guatemala, Ak'abal has published twelve books of poetry. His work reflects the oral tradition of the Mayan K'ikche' from Guatemala and Central America. Ak'abal is world-renowned for his poetic use of onomatopoeia. His work has been translated into several languages and has been recognized internationally. He won the Blaise Cendrars Award in 1997 and was honored with the Canto de América Award by UNESCO in Mexico in 1998.

Óscar Alfaro (1921-1963) Alfaro was a poet, narrator and educator born in Bolivia, where he was regarded as "the children's poet." He worked intensively to promote children's literature. His books include *Cajita de música*, *Alfabeto de estrellas*, *Cien poemas para niños* and *La escuela de fiesta*.

Miguel Ángel Asturias (1899-1974) Born in Guatemala, Asturias was a prominent poet and novelist. In 1925 he translated the Mayan bible *Popol Vuh*, into Spanish. He published prodigiously; and some of his most popular books are *Leyendas de Guatemala*, *El señor presidente* and *Hombres de maíz*, which is considered his masterpiece. He won the Nobel Prize for Literature in 1967.

Germán Berdiales (1896-1975) Born in Argentina, Berdiales was a poet, writer and teacher. He explored all genres of children's literature. Some of his most popular books are *Joyitas*, *Fabulario*, *El nené en su corralito*, *Cielo pequeñito* and *Mis versos para la escuela*. He also published many plays for children.

Julia de Burgos (1914-1953) Her full name was Julia Constancia Burgos García. Born in Puerto Rico, Burgos was a schoolteacher, poet and journalist. She chose to live in exile in Cuba and the United States, and died in Harlem, New York, where she was buried anonymously in a common grave. Her most popular books are *Poemas en veinte surcos*, *Canción de la verdad sencilla* and *El mar y tú*. Her poems reflect her lonely life and her profound love of nature.

Víctor Eduardo Caro (1877-1944) Caro was a poet, writer and journalist born in Colombia. He published *A la sombra del alero*, *Sonetos* and *La juventud de Don Miguel Antonio Caro* and *Los números: su historia, sus propiedades, sus mentiras y verdades*.

Carlos F. Changmarín (1922-) Born in Panama, Changmarín studied education, painting and journalism and worked as a teacher. Some of his most popular books are *Socavón*, *Dos poemas*, *Poemas corporales*, *Versos del pueblo* and *Versos de muchachita*. He also wrote novels and published two collections of children's poetry, *Noche buena mala* and *La muñeca de tusa*.

David Chericián (1940-) Chericián was born in Cuba. During his youth he worked as an actor in theater, radio and television. Later he worked as chief editor for several magazines. A few well-known composers have written music for his poems. Chericián was awarded the Premio Nacional Cubano de la Crítica in 1983 for his book *Junto aquí poemas de amor*.

Teresa Crespo de Salvador (1928-) A poet and narrator, Crespo is one of the most prominent figures of children's literature in Ecuador. She has published *Rondas*, *Pepe Golondrina*, *Hilván de sueños*, *Novena del Niño Jesús*, *Mateo Zimbaña* and *Ana de los ríos*.

Maya Cu (1968-) Born in Guatemala, Cu has published her work in magazines, newspapers and anthologies. Her first book, *Poemaya*, was published in 1996.

Roque Dalton (1935-1975) Born in El Salvador, Dalton had a short life but published extensively. *La Ventana en el rostro* was his first book and, along with his collection of poems, *Taberna y otros lugares*, won the Casa de las Américas Award in 1969. Dalton published *Miguel Mármol*, a study of the 1932 peasants' insurrection in El Salvador, as well as a collage-novel called *Pobrecito poeta que era yo*.

Rubén Darío (1867-1916) Born in Nicaragua, Darío was a modernist poet who changed the path of Latin American poetry. His full name was Félix Rubén García Sarmiento. He published extensively and many of his poems, stories and articles have been translated into English, French, Italian, Portuguese, German and Scandinavian.

Carolina Escobar Sarti (1960-) Escobar Sarti is a writer, poet and teacher born in Guatemala. In 1978 she won the Festival de la Primavera Award for her journal publications and in 2000 the UNICEF Award in Communication. She has published two collections of poems, *La penúltima luz* and *Palabras sonámbulas*, and since 1993 more than three hundred articles and essays in newspapers as well as national and international magazines.

Alfredo Espino (1900-1928) Espino was born in El Salvador. His ninety-six poems were published after his death in 1930 in a collection called *Jícaras tristes*, which became a literary treasure for many people in El Salvador.

Julia Esquivel (1930-) A Guatemalan poet and theologian, Esquivel has worked with human rights organizations for many years. Her first book of poetry, *Amenazado de resurrección* was translated into English as *Threatened with Resurrection*; and her second book, *Florecerás Guatemal*, appeared in translation as *The Certainty of Spring*.

Francisco Feliciano Sánchez (1950-) Born in Puerto Rico, Feliciano Sánchez is an educator, librarian and director of the Educational Workshop Aspira. He has worked to improve and promote education for children from low-income families, and to promote college education for minority groups. He published *Los poemarios místicos, Del lenguaje de la piedra* and *Enén: el barquito de papel*.

Emilia Gallego Alfonso (1946-) Gallego Alfonso was born in Cuba. In 1981 she won the Children's Literature Award given by the Universidad de La Habana, Cuba, Department of Cultural Affairs, for her collection of poems *Para un niño travieso*. She went on to win the Cuban National Poetry Award, La Edad de Oro, for her books *Y dice una mariposa* (1981) and *Sol sin prisa* (1985).

Otto Raúl González (1921-) A prolific Guatemalan poet, narrator and essayist, González has published more than thirty-five books. Some of his most popular titles are *Voz y Voto del geranio, A fuego lento, El hombre de las lámparas celestes* and *La siesta del gorila y otros poemas*. His work explores social themes critically but with a subtle symbolism.

Nicolás Guillén (1902-1989) Guillén was born in Cuba. His first poems were written in the 1930s, and he became the most prominent figure of Afroantillean poetry. His writings for journals have been collected in *Prosa deprisa*. His later poems, published in *Poemas para niños y mayores de edad*, reflect social and political themes.

Julio Herrera y Reissig (1875-1910) Herrera y Reissig was an Uruguayan poet who became the leader of modernism in his country. His complete works, *Obras completas* (1911-1913), were published posthumously.

Juana de Ibarbourou (1895-1979) Ibarbourou was an Uruguayan writer and member of the Academia uruguaya. She won the country's first national award for literature in 1959. Known as "Juana of the Americas," she published many books and works for children such as *Ejemplario, Libro de lectura* and *Los sueños de Natacha*.

Claudia Lars (1899-1974) Claudia Lars was the pen name of Carmen Brannon, a writer born in El Salvador. Her book *Estrellas en el pozo* included a section dedicated to her son. In 1955 she published a collection of poems called *Escuela de pájaros* that has become a classic of children's literature in El Salvador. She was also the author of the anthology for children entitled *Girasol* and wrote her memoirs in *Tierra de infancia*.

Ismael Lee Vallejo (1932-) Born in Colombia, Lee Vallejo is a member of the Iberoamerican Academy of Letters, Arts and Science. He collaborated with the newspapers *El Siglo* and *El Espectador* and, as a young writer, published editorials in the newspaper *La Patria*. His works include *Treinta manuscritos al amor, Caricaturas de perfil y de frente* and *El cuero*.

Marcos Leibovich Little is known about this poet, even though the poem "*Con sol y con luna*" is popular throughout Latin America.

Carmen Lyra (1888-1948) Carmen Lyra was the pen name of the Costa Rican poet María Isabel Carvajal Quesada. She was an intellectual who promoted education and art for young people, and was the author of the classic children's book, *Los cuentos de mi tía Panchita*. She was a professor of Children's Literature at the Instituto Normal de Heredia in Costa Rica and later lived in exile, in Mexico, until her death.

Gabriela Mistral (1889-1957) Born Lucila Godoy de Alcayaga in Chile, she was a rural schoolteacher and a recipient of the Nobel Prize for Literature in 1945, the only Latin American woman ever to be named a Nobel laureate. By 1917, she was a respected published poet in Chile. In 1922, Mistral published a collection of stories entitled *Lecturas para Mujeres* and *Desolación,* her first book of poetry. She was a prolific writer and published *Ternura, Tala* and *Lagar,* among many other books.

Amado Nervo (1870-1919) Nervo was once considered the most important modernist Mexican poet. He studied science, philosophy and law, and his first book of poems, *Místicas,* was published in 1898. Nervo was a diplomat and a correspondent for several Mexican journals. In his poetry, he subtly weaves patriotic themes with art and love.

Esther María Ossés (1914-) A poet and educator born in Panama, Ossés has lived in Argentina, Guatemala and Venezuela. She has worked to promote literary groups; and some of her poetry books for children are *Crece y camina, La niña y el mar* and *Soles de Maracaibo*.

Nicanor Parra (1914-) Born in Chile, Parra has published many books, including one with his compatriot Pablo Neruda. His first book, *Cancionero sin nombre,* was published in 1938. He was a professor of theoretical physics at the Universidad de Chile and has taught in several universities in the United States. Parra has read his poems in England, France, Russia, the United States, Mexico and Cuba.

Octavio Paz (1914-1999) Paz was a prolific Mexican poet and writer. He worked hard to promote culture and founded several highly regarded literary magazines. He was a scholar, a journalist and a leading writer in Latin America. His work was recognized in 1990, when he was awarded the Nobel Prize for Literature. Paz explored diverse themes in his writings but some of his best-known subjects are Mexican anthropology and literary theory.

Rafael Pombo (1883-1912) Pombo was a poet, translator and fabulist born in Colombia, where he is considered a classic author of children's literature. His books, *Cuentos pintados* and *Cuentos morales para niños formales* are full of humor, fantasy and moral values.

Aramís Quintero (1948-) Quintero is a poet, narrator and essayist who was born in Cuba. He studied Hispanic Literature at the Universidad de La Habana and has published more than fifteen books. He was awarded the Cuban National Prize, La Edad de Oro, for his children's book, *Días de aire,* in 1982 and for his book for young adults, *Maíz regado,* in 1983. *Fábulas y estampas* and *Letras mágicas* number among his other books for children.

Manuel Felipe Rugeles (1903-1959) Rugeles was a prominent Venezuelan writer and founder of the children's magazine *Pico-Pico*. His book *Canta Pirulero* is considered a classic of Venezuelan children's literature. Other popular books are *Canto a Iberoamérica, Cantos del sur al norte* and *Dorada estación,* which was published posthumously.

Clarisa Ruiz (1955-) Born in Colombia, Ruiz studied Social Communication at the Universidad Jorge Tadeo Lozano, then studied philosophy at the Universidad Nacional de Bogotá and the Sorbonne in Paris. She has worked extensively to promote the arts in Colombia. Her books for children include *Traba la lengua la traba, Palabras que me gustan, El libro de los días* and *El gato con botas.*

Excilia Saldaña (1946-1999) Saldaña was a Cuban essayist, poet and author. *Cantos para un mayito una paloma* won the Premio Nacional de Literatura Infantil Ismaelillo in 1979, and *La noche* was awarded the same prize in 1989. In 1987 she published *Kele-kele,* a collection of narratives for young adults, inspired by Yoruban mythology.

Enrique Solano Rodríguez (1940-) Solano Rodríguez is a poet and editor who was born in Peru. He is currently director of the Peruvian Association of Children's Literature and has edited many books, including *Agonías rebeldes, Sonajas de paz y otros poemas, Poetas a los niños de América* and *Definiciones y otros poemas.*

Alfonsina Storni (1892-1938) Storni was born in Switzerland but her family moved to Argentina when she was very young. Writing under the pen name Tao Lao, she became a popular poet in Argentina. She also worked as a teacher and journalist.

Froilán Turcios (1875-1943) Turcios was born in Honduras. He founded the weekly newspaper *El Pensamiento,* was director of the weekly newspaper *El Tiempo* and of the magazine of arts and letters *Esfinge*. Appointed to various political positions and embassies for Honduras, he worked hard to promote literature among young people in his country.

Irene Vasco (1952-) Born in Colombia, Vasco is the founder and co-director of Espantapájaros Taller. She has worked to promote reading in neighborhood libraries and recreation centers for children and young adults from low-income families. She has translated Lygia Bojunga, Ana María Machado and Rubem Fonseca from the Portuguese. Her books include *Como todos los días, Paso a paso, Conjuros y sortilegios* and *Don Salomón y la peluquera.*

Javier Villegas Fernández (1955-) Born in Peru, Villegas Fernández won the Premio Nacional de Educacíon "Horacio" in 1991 for his book *La luna cantora*. He received a special mention from the Biblioteca Nacional del Perú and is the director of the Centro de Promoción de la Literatura Infantil y la Lectura. He is also the director and editor of the magazine *Poroporo*. His other books include *Rimando la alegría, Repertorio de ternura, La flauta del agua* and *Poesía para niños.*

María Elena Walsh (1930-) Walsh is a prominent Argentinean writer, composer and singer. In 1947, at the age of seventeen, Walsh edited her first book of poetry *Otoño imperdonable*. Her prolific body of work includes songs, poems, plays, movies and recitals. She has been honored with various national and international awards and was named an illustrious citizen of Buenos Aires. Her books have been translated into eight languages.

INDEX OF POETS

Ak'abal, Humberto (Guatemala)
   Key, The 59
   Little Boat, The 53
   Messengers of the Rain 36
   Rain 52
   Traveler, The 25
   Tukumux Bird, The 26
Alfaro, Óscar (Bolivia)
   Fuchsias 39
Anonymous, attributed to Jorge Luis Borges
   Farewell 74
Araucano traditional (Chile)
   Chief Koruinka's Song 13
Asturias, Miguel Ángel (Guatemala)
   Plenty 71
Berdiales, Germán (Argentina)
   Tomorrow Sunday 23
Burgos, Julia de (Puerto Rico)
   Sea Wall, A 65
Caro, Víctor Eduardo (Colombia)
   This Said Chiras the Chicken 41
Changmarín, Carlos F. (Panama)
   Black Man from Panama 60
Chericián, David (Cuba)
   Magician, The 50
Crespo de Salvador, Teresa (Ecuador)
   Song 11
Cu, Maya (Guatemala)
   Mayo 40
Dalton, Roque (El Salvador)
   To Achieve Peace 66
Darío, Rubén (Nicaragua)
   Morning Routine 64
   Tropic 14
Escobar Sarti, Carolina (Guatemala)
   Girl Stories 18
Espino, Alfredo (El Salvador)
   Nest, The 38
Esquivel, Julia (Guatemala)
   Resurrection 37
Feliciano Sánchez, Francisco (Puerto Rico)
   Boats and Dreams 70
Gallego Alfonso, Emilia (Cuba)
   In the Garden 33
   Little Weaving Spider, The 44
   Sea Shell, The 49
González, Otto Raúl (Guatemala)
   Sign of the Geranium I 45
   Sign of the Geranium II 45
Guaraní traditional (Paraguay)
   Morning Prayer to the Creator 16

Guillén, Nicolás (Cuba)
   Wall, The 48
Herrera y Reissig, Julio (Uruguay)
   Land of My Birth 62
Ibarbourou, Juana de, (Uruguay)
   Summer 17
Lars, Claudia (El Salvador)
   Kite, The 24
Lee Vallejo, Ismael (Colombia)
   José Manuel 25
Leibovich, Marcos (Argentina)
   With the Sun and the Moon 49
Lyra, Carmen (Costa Rica)
   Little Dandelion, The 71
Mistral, Gabriela (Chile)
   Give Me Your Hand 12
   Lady Spring 31
Náhuatl traditional, Fragment (Mexico)
   Icnocuicatl 27
Natives from the island of Tiburón (Mexico)
   Mother Whale 34
Nervo, Amado (Mexico)
   Squirrel, The 33
Ossés, Esther María (Panama)
   From Where the Rose? 30
Parra, Nicanor (Chile)
   Questions Around Tea Time 63
Paz, Octavio (Mexico)
   At the Water's Edge 56
   Example 57
Pombo, Rafael (Colombia)
   Poor Little Old Lady, The 72
   Tale of the Wandering Tadpole 20
Quintero, Aramís (Cuba)
   Firefly 50
   Indian Canoes 46
   Rider, The 32
   Rivulet 70
Rugeles, Manuel Felipe (Venezuela)
   Little Tortoise, The 34
   This Child Don Simón 68
Ruiz, Clarisa (Colombia)
   Watercolor 51
Saldaña, Excilia (Cuba)
   Castles 46
Solano Rodríguez, Enrique (Peru)
   Little Moon, Look, Run Over Here, Come 17
Storni, Alfonsina (Argentina)
   We Will Go to the Mountain 40
Traditional (Brazil and Latin America)
   Rice Pudding 10

Turcios, Froilán (Honduras)
  Coyolares, The (Palm Trees) 35
Vasco, Irene (Colombia)
  Magic Potion for All Kinds of Uses 47

Villegas Fernández, Javier (Peru)
  Frog and the Moon, The 39
Walsh, María Elena (Argentina)
  Sun Has No Pockets, The 58
  Wartime Postcard 69

INDEX OF TITLES

At the Water's Edge, Octavio Paz (Mexico) 56
Black Man from Panama, Carlos F. Changmarín (Panama) 60
Boats and Dreams, Francisco Feliciano Sánchez (Puerto Rico) 70
Castles, Excilia Saldaña (Cuba) 46
Chief Koruinka's Song, Araucano traditional (Chile) 13
Coyolares, The, Froilán Turcios (Honduras) 35
Example, Octavio Paz (Mexico) 57
Farewell, Anonymous 74
Firefly, Aramís Quintero (Cuba) 50
Frog and the Moon, The, Javier Villegas Fernández (Peru) 39
From Where the Rose?, Esther María Ossés (Panama) 30
Fuchsias, Óscar Alfaro (Bolivia) 39
Girl Stories, Carolina Escobar Sarti (Guatemala) 18
Give Me Your Hand, Gabriela Mistral (Chile) 12
Icnocuicatl, Náhuatl traditional (Mexico) 27
In the Garden, Emilia Gallego Alfonso (Cuba) 33
Indian Canoes, Aramís Quintero (Cuba) 46
José Manuel, Ismael Lee Vallejo (Colombia) 25
Key, The, Humberto Ak'abal (Guatemala) 59
Kite, The, Claudia Lars (El Salvador) 24
Lady Spring, Gabriela Mistral (Chile) 31
Land of My Birth, Julio Herrera y Reissig (Uruguay) 62
Little Boat, The, Humberto Ak'abal (Guatemala) 53
Little Dandelion, The, Carmen Lyra (Costa Rica) 71
Little Moon, Look, Run Over Here, Come, Enrique Solano Rodríguez (Peru) 17
Little Tortoise, The, Manuel Felipe Rugeles (Venezuela) 34
Little Weaving Spider, The, Emilia Gallego Alfonso (Cuba) 44
Magic Potion for All Kinds of Uses, Irene Vasco (Colombia) 47
Magician, The, David Chericián (Cuba) 50
Mayo, Maya Cu (Guatemala) 40
Messengers of the Rain, Humberto Ak'abal (Guatemala) 36
Morning Prayer to the Creator, Guaraní traditional (Paraguay) 16
Morning Routine, Rubén Darío (Nicaragua) 64

Mother Whale, Natives from the island of Tiburón (Mexico) 34
Nest, The, Alfredo Espino (El Salvador) 38
Plenty, Miguel Ángel Asturias (Guatemala) 71
Poor Little Old Lady, The, Rafael Pombo (Colombia) 72
Questions Around Tea Time, Nicanor Parra (Chile) 63
Rain, Humberto Ak'abal (Guatemala) 52
Resurrection, Julia Esquivel (Guatemala) 37
Rice Pudding, traditional (Brazil and Latin America) 10
Rider, The, Aramís Quintero (Cuba) 32
Rivulet, Aramís Quintero (Cuba) 70
Sea Shell, The, Emilia Gallego Alfonso (Cuba) 49
Sea Wall, A, Julia de Burgos (Puerto Rico) 65
Sign of the Geranium I, Otto Raúl González (Guatemala) 45
Sign of the Geranium II, Otto Raúl González (Guatemala) 45
Song, Teresa Crespo de Salvador (Ecuador) 11
Squirrel, The, Amado Nervo (Mexico) 33
Summer, Juana de Ibarbourou (Uruguay) 17
Sun Has No Pockets, The, María Elena Walsh (Argentina) 58
Tale of the Wandering Tadpole, Rafael Pombo (Colombia) 20
This Child Don Simón, Manuel Felipe Rugeles (Venezuela) 68
This Said Chiras the Chicken, Víctor Eduardo Caro (Colombia) 41
To Achieve Peace, Roque Dalton (El Salvador) 66
Tomorrow Sunday, Germán Berdiales (Argentina) 23
Traveler, The, Humberto Ak'abal (Guatemala) 25
Tropic, Rubén Darío (Nicaragua) 14
Tukumux Bird, The, Humberto Ak'abal (Guatemala) 26
Wall, The, Nicolás Guillén (Cuba) 48
Wartime Postcard, María Elena Walsh (Argentina) 69
Watercolor, Clarisa Ruiz (Colombia) 51
We Will Go to the Mountain, Alfonsina Storni (Argentina) 40
With the Sun and the Moon, Marcos Leibovich (Argentina) 49